WHAT DOES IT FEEL LIKE TO BE SCARED?

Think of a time when you felt scared. Maybe you climbed a tree and didn't know how to get back down. Has a big dog ever growled at you? How did you feel?

When you are scared, your heart beats fast. Your lips might **quiver**. You may cover your eyes or ears. You may want to run away from the person or thing that made you feel that way.

USING YOUR SENSES

You have five **senses**. Each of your senses makes you feel something. People can touch, taste, see, smell, and hear. Seeing a monster in a movie might make you feel scared. Hearing loud thunder during a storm can be scary too.

TALKING ABOUT YOUR FEELINGS

Talking about how you feel is important. If you feel scared, find a trusted grown-up. This person can help you. You can tell them about your scared feelings.

Sometimes it's tough to talk about your feelings. But keep trying! Use your words to explain the emotion you feel on the inside. Let your inside feelings out.

UNDERSTANDING FEELING SCARED

Different things are scary to different people. If someone near you uses a loud or angry voice, you might feel scared. Having to get a shot at the doctor's office can be scary too.

When you are scared, you might feel like you want to cry. It may feel like something is stuck in your throat.

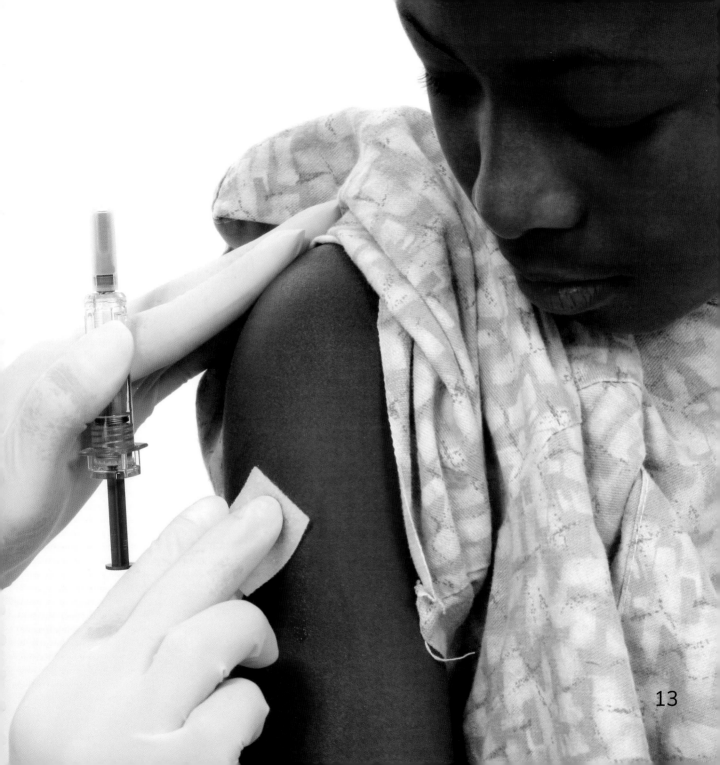

13

Being scared is a normal way to feel sometimes. But the longer you are scared, the bigger those feelings can grow. It might be hard to **concentrate**. You might not want to try new things.

Next time you feel scared, try to think about why you feel that way. Then use words to talk your scared feelings out. Now, new calm feelings can come in!

HANDLING YOUR FEELINGS

You can learn how to handle your feelings. Feeling scared sometimes is normal. Being scared for a long time is not a good feeling. You won't want to miss out on trying new things because you are scared.

Try to remember what scared you. Then tell a grown-up you trust. Being **brave** enough to talk about feeling scared will make you feel better.

You can help a scared friend.
Ask why they are scared. Listen.
Share with them a time when you
were scared. Remind your friend of
something they do that is brave.
Talking about feelings is a brave thing.

MINDFULNESS ACTIVITY

Count down 5, 4, 3, 2, 1. Use your five senses to focus and relax.

What You Do:

1. Find a quiet room or a spot outside.

2. Take a deep breath.

3. Name **5** objects you can see.

4. Find **4** objects you can touch and feel.

5. Can you name **3** different sounds you hear?

6. Now, try to name **2** things you smell.

7. Last, describe the taste of **1** favorite food.

GLOSSARY

brave (BRAYV)—showing courage and willingness to do difficult things

concentrate (KAHN-suhn-trayt)—to focus your thoughts and attention on something

emotion (i-MOH-shuhn)—a strong feeling; people have and show emotions such as happiness, sadness, fear, anger, and jealousy

quiver (KWIV-ur)—to move with a slight shaking motion

sense (SENSS)—a way of knowing about your surroundings; hearing, smelling, touching, tasting, and sight are the five senses

READ MORE

Beattie, Amy. *When I Feel Scared*. New York: Enslow Publishing, 2020.

Carbone, Courtney. *This Makes Me Scared*. New York: Random House Children's Books, 2018.

Devera, Czeena. *Fear*. Ann Arbor, MI: Cherry Lake Publishing, 2021.

INTERNET SITES

KidsHealth: Talking About Your Feelings
kidshealth.org/en/kids/talk-feelings.html

PBS Kids: When Something Scary Happens
pbskids.org/learn/when-something-scary-happens/

INDEX

ABOUT THE AUTHOR

Nicole A. Mansfield is passionate about writing books for children. She loves to exercise and to sing at church. She lives with her husband and three children on a military base in Georgia.